Lara Ladybug

Written by Christine Florie
Illustrated by Danny Brooks Dalby

Children's Press®
A Division of Scholastic Inc.
New York • Toronto • London • Auckland • Sydney
Mexico City • New Delhi • Hong Kong
Danbury, Connecticut

Dear Parents/Educators,

Welcome to Rookie Ready to Learn. Each Rookie Reader in this series includes additional age-appropriate Let's Learn Together activity pages that help your young child to be better prepared when starting school. *Lara Ladybug* offers opportunities for you and your child to talk about the important social/emotional skill of persistence.

Here are early-learning skills you and your child will encounter in the *Lara Ladybug* Let's Learn Together pages:

• Counting
• Same and different
• Vocabulary

We hope you enjoy sharing this delightful, enhanced reading experience with your early learner.

Library of Congress Cataloging-in-Publication Data

Florie, Christine, 1964-
  Lara Ladybug / written by Christine Florie ; illustrated by Danny Brooks Dalby.
    p. cm. -- (Rookie ready to learn)
  Summary: A ladybug searches all over for her lost spots. Includes suggested learning activities.
  ISBN 978-0-531-26417-1-- ISBN 978-0-531-26698-4 (pbk.)
  [1. Lost and found possessions--Fiction. 2. Ladybugs--Fiction.] I. Dalby, Danny
Brooks, ill. II. Title. III. Series.
  PZ7.F6646Lar 2011
  [E]--dc22
                              2010049991

CHILDREN'S PRESS, and ROOKIE READY TO LEARN, and associated logos are trademarks and or registered trademarks of Scholastic Library Publishing. SCHOLASTIC and associated logos are trademarks or registered trademarks of Scholastic, Inc.

1 2 3 4 5 6 7 8 9 10 R 18 17 16 15 14 13 12 11

Lara Ladybug lost her spots.
Where can they be?

3

Did she leave them in her garden?
Let's see.

Lara Ladybug lost her spots.
Where can they be?

8

Did she leave them by the lake?
Let's see.

Lara Ladybug lost her spots.
Where can they be?

Did she leave them under the tree?
Let's see.

Lara stopped to rest.
What did she see?

Her spots!

One

Two

Three

Congratulations!

You just finished reading *Lara Ladybug* and learned how important it is to not give up when something means a lot to you.

About the Author
Christine Florie is a children's book editor and writer. When not editing and writing, she enjoys traveling, visiting sunny beaches, and spending time with family and friends.

About the Illustrator
Danny Brooks Dalby has been drawing his entire life. His motto is "Read all of your books, eat all of your vegetables, and love your mother."

Lara Ladybug

Let's learn together!

I am a Ladybug

(Sing this song to the tune of "This is the Way.")

I am a ladybug, black and red.
I have a body, six legs, and a head.
Watch me use my wings
To fly from the ground.
My antennae help me get around.

Rookie
READY TO
LEARN

Spot the Difference

Lara had to carefully look in different places before she found her spots. Now you look carefully at these two pictures. Point to three things that are different in the second picture.

PARENT TIP: Ask your child if he remembers any of the places Lara had to explore before she found her spots. This can lead to a talk with your child about the different surroundings he experiences each day: his room, your backyard, your neighborhood block. Together, make a list of what you both observe about these different places.

27

How Many?

Lara is happy to find her spots.
She has fun counting them: 1, 2, 3. You can have fun counting the things in this picture.

1. Count how many 🪰 there are.
dragonflies

2. Count how many 🌼 you see.
flowers

3. Count how many are buzzing around.

bees

4. Count how many are in the sky.

clouds

Lost and Found

Lara Ladybug lost her spots. She looked and looked until she found them. Follow the path with your finger to help Lara Ladybug find her spots.

PARENT TIP: After helping Lara find her spots, take this opportunity to talk to your child about how she felt when she lost something and then found it. Ask: "How do you think Lara Ladybug feels about losing her spots?" You might also want to discuss how Lara doesn't give up — and ultimately finds her spots.

Ladybug Potato Print

Create your own ladybug with special spots.

YOU WILL NEED: A potato, cut in half

Paper **Finger paints** **or food coloring**

Markers

1 Dip a potato half in red finger paint or food coloring. Place the potato on paper to make a print of the ladybug's body.

2 When the paint is dry, draw a line down the middle to make two wings.

3 Decorate each wing with the same number of spots as your age. Draw a face and add the antennae.

Lara Ladybug Word List (29 Words)

be	lake	she	tree
by	Lara	spots	two
can	leave	stopped	under
did	let's	the	what
garden	lost	them	where
her	one	they	
in	rest	three	
ladybug	see	to	

PARENT TIP: Ask your child: "What letter do *Lara* and *ladybug* start with?" Together, find the other *L* words on the list above. Write those words on a separate sheet of paper. Look for things that start with *L* in your home or your child's room. Add those to your list. Then add other *L* words to your list: *lion*, *library*, *lake*, and so on.